BIG
CHICKENS

LESLIE HELAKOSKI ❋ illustrated by HENRY COLE

SCHOLASTIC INC.

New York Toronto London Auckland Sydney
Mexico City New Delhi Hong Kong Buenos Aires

ISBN-13: 978-0-439-02613-0
ISBN-10: 0-439-02613-X

Text copyright © 2006 by Leslie Helakoski. Illustrations copyright © 2006 by Henry Cole. All rights reserved. Published by Scholastic Inc., 557 Broadway, New York, NY 10012, by arrangement with Dutton Children's Books, a division of Penguin Young Readers Group, a member of Penguin Group (USA) Inc. SCHOLASTIC and associated logos are trademarks and/or registered trademarks of Scholastic Inc.

12 11 10 9 8 7 6 5 4 3 2 1   7 8 9 10 11 12/0

Printed in the U.S.A.   08

First Scholastic printing, March 2007

Designed by Heather Wood

To Beth,
the bravest chick I know
—L.H.

For Tweetybird,
who is never a big chicken!
—H.C.

ONE DAY four big chickens peeked out the coop window and saw a wolf sneak into the farmyard.

The chickens pwocked, flocked, and rocked. They knocked into themselves and each other until one by one they tumbled out of the coop. The door slammed shut, and the chickens ran into the woods to hide.

After a while, it became very
quiet.

"I'm afraid to go home," said
one chicken.

"Ohh . . . " said the others.

"Me too."

"Me three."

"Me four." So four cautious,
careful, cowardly, chicken
chickens walked deeper into the
woods until . . .

. . . they came to a deep ditch.

"I'm afraid to jump," said one chicken.

"Ohh . . ." said the others.

"Me too."

"Me three."

"Me four."

"What if we can't jump that far?"

"What if we fall in the ditch?"

"What if we get sucked into the mud?"

The chickens tutted, putted, and flutted. They butted into themselves and each other, until one by one . . .

. . . they fell into the ditch.

The chickens landed smack
in the mud. Feet flew out from
under, and bottoms flipped over.
Bodies plucked up, and mud
sucked down. Legs sank in.
Necks stretched out. Until . . .

. . . their chicken feet grabbed
some roots, and they pulled
themselves out of the ditch.

Four dirty chickens came to a
cow pasture. "I'm afraid of cows,"
said one chicken.

"Ohh . . ." said the others.

"Me too."

"Me three."

"Me four."

"What if the cows chase us?"

"What if we get poked with
their horns?"

"What if we step in a cow
patty?"

The chickens squeaked,
squirmed, and squealed. They
squawked at themselves and
each other, until one by one . . .

. . . they bumped into the cows.

The chickens ran, and the
cows chased. The cows stomped
down, and the chickens fluttered
up. Horns dipped under, and legs
leaped over. Tongues hung out.
Feet squished in. Until . . .

. . . their chicken wings flapped, and they flopped over the fence to the other side.

Four dusty chickens came to a lake. "I'm afraid of the water," said one chicken.

"Ohh . . ." said the others.

"Me too."

"Me three."

"Me four."

"What if the boat sinks?"

"What if we fall in the lake?"

"What if we hit an iceberg?"

The chickens sputtered, shuddered, and muttered. They fluttered into themselves and each other, until . . .

. . . the boat tipped, and one by one they fell out.

The chickens landed in the lake with a splash. The boat went down, and their toes pointed up. Heads bobbed under, and waves swept over. Breath sucked in. Water squirted out. Until . . .

. . . they grabbed onto a log, and their chicken legs kicked all the way to shore.

Four drippy chickens spied a cave. "I'm afraid of caves," said one chicken.

"Ohh . . ." said the others.

"Me too."

"Me three."

"Me four."

"What if we can't see in there?"

"What if we wake up some bats?"

"What if we fall into a bottomless pit?"

The four chickens flurried, hurried, and worried. They scurried into themselves and each other, until one by one . . .

. . . they stumbled into the cave.

The chickens bumped into walls. Rocks rolled over, and toes crunched under. Bats flew down, and chickens swatted up. Dark closed in. Eyes bulged out. Until . . .

. . . their chicken ears heard a noise in back of the cave, and they grew very quiet.

Four dazed chickens listened to a long, low growl. "I'm afraid of growls," said one chicken.

"Ohh . . ." said the others.

"Me too."

"Me three."

"Me four."

"What if it's a big animal?"

"What if it's a big, hairy animal?"

"What if it's a big, hairy, chicken-chomping animal?"

Something crawled from the back of the cave. It was big. It was hairy. It looked at the chickens and licked its lips.

"It's a wolf!"

The chickens picked, pecked,
and pocked. They ruffled,
puffled, and shuffled. They
shrieked, squeaked, and freaked,
until . . .

. . . the wolf ran out of the cave.

Their chicken hearts soared.
"I am a big, brave chicken,"
said one chicken.
"Ohh . . ." said the others.
"Me too."
"Me three."
"Me four."
"We have chicken power."
"We have chicken brains."
"We have chicken guts."

"Yes," they all agreed, "we are very big chickens."
Four dirty, dusty, drippy, dazed, daring chickens
strutted all the way home.